May the Lord bless you and keep you.

May the Lord show you His kindness.

May He have mercy on you.

May the Lord watch over you and give you peace.

Numbers 6:24-27 (ICB)

tiger tales

5 River Road, Suite 128, Wilton, CT 06897
Published in the United States 2015
This edition published in the United States 2016
Text by Becky Davies
Text copyright © 2015 Little Tiger Press
Illustrations copyright © 2004, 2006, 2007,
2008, 2009, 2015 Tina Macnaughton
ISBN-13: 978-1-68010-023-5
ISBN-10: 1-68010-023-8
Printed in China
LTP/1400/1353/1015
All rights reserved
10 9 8 7 6 5 4 3 2 1

For more insight and activities, visit us at www.tigertalesbooks.com

Bedtime Blessing

by Becky Davies

Illustrated by Tina Macnaughton

tiger tales

As the sun sinks gently
in the glowing sky,
God is watching over
from His place on high.

Lambs play one last game
in the fading light,
Knowing He will guard them
closely through the night.

He protects and guides us.
He hears all our prayers.
Every living creature
is safe in His care.

In icy lands the penguins

huddle up so tight.

He keeps them warm and snug,

in swirling mists of white.

As sleepy kittens gather
at the close of day,
He smiles to hear them purring,
tired from their play.

Every bird is special—
He made each one unique.

They sing of God's great blessing
before they go to sleep.

Happy, sleepy hippos
cuddle up to rest,
Snuggling as night falls
on our world so blessed.

He watches as the puppies
settle down to doze.
Gentle dreams are waiting
for little eyes to close.

Giraffes gather together
to sleep on sheltered ground.
Nestled up 'til morning,
they'll be safe and sound.

Silver stars shine brightly
in the sky above,
Each one a reminder
of His eternal love.

Sleep safely now, my little one,
'til night becomes the day,
For God will be there by your side
to guide you on your way.

Each of us is cherished,
from big to very small.
We are all His creatures—
God bless us one and all.